# a DOT in the SNOW

For our dot in the snow — C. A.

For Mum and Dad — F. W.

UNIVERSITY PRESS

Great Clarendon Street, Oxford OX2 6DP

Oxford University Press is a department of the University of Oxford.
It furthers the University's objective of excellence in research, scholarship,
and education by publishing worldwide. Oxford is a registered trade mark of
Oxford University Press in the UK and in certain other countries

British Library Cataloguing in Publication Data available

ISBN: 978-0-19-274426-5 (hardback)

1 3 5 7 9 10 8 6 4 2

Printed in China

Paper used in the production of this book is a natural, recyclable product made
from wood grown in sustainable forests. The manufacturing process conforms
to the environmental regulations of the country of origin

# a D**O**T in the SNOW

Corrinne Averiss        Fiona Woodcock

**OXFORD**

UNIVERSITY PRESS

Miki wanted Mum to play in the snow,
not fish on the ice.

Snow was soft,
and fishing looked hard.
Miki wasn't ready to dive.

So he scampered away.

Up, up, up the snowy ridge.

And that's when he saw it . . .
a dot in the snow.

He raced to get a closer look.

The Dot waved its paw.

Miki sniffed.
It smelled friendly.

He liked its
twinkly face.

And the gurgling
sound it made.

Did the Dot want to play?

Yes, it did!

And then suddenly, it didn't.

A red thing was missing
from one of the Dot's paws.

Miki raced back, the ice went creak-crack!

The red thing fell into the sea. Miki dived!

The deeper it sank,
the harder he paddled.

Until he caught it!

Now the ice
was breaking everywhere.

Miki showed the Dot
how to jump.

And together they climbed,
up, up, up
to the place where they played.

But where had it gone?
Everything was white.

Everything except for . . .


a dot in the snow.

A Mummy Dot!

Two cold noses nudged goodbye.

And twinkly faces hugged hello.
Miki knew he would miss the Dot . . .

But he missed his Mum even more.

Paw after paw,
slow through the snow,
Miki marched back to the ice.

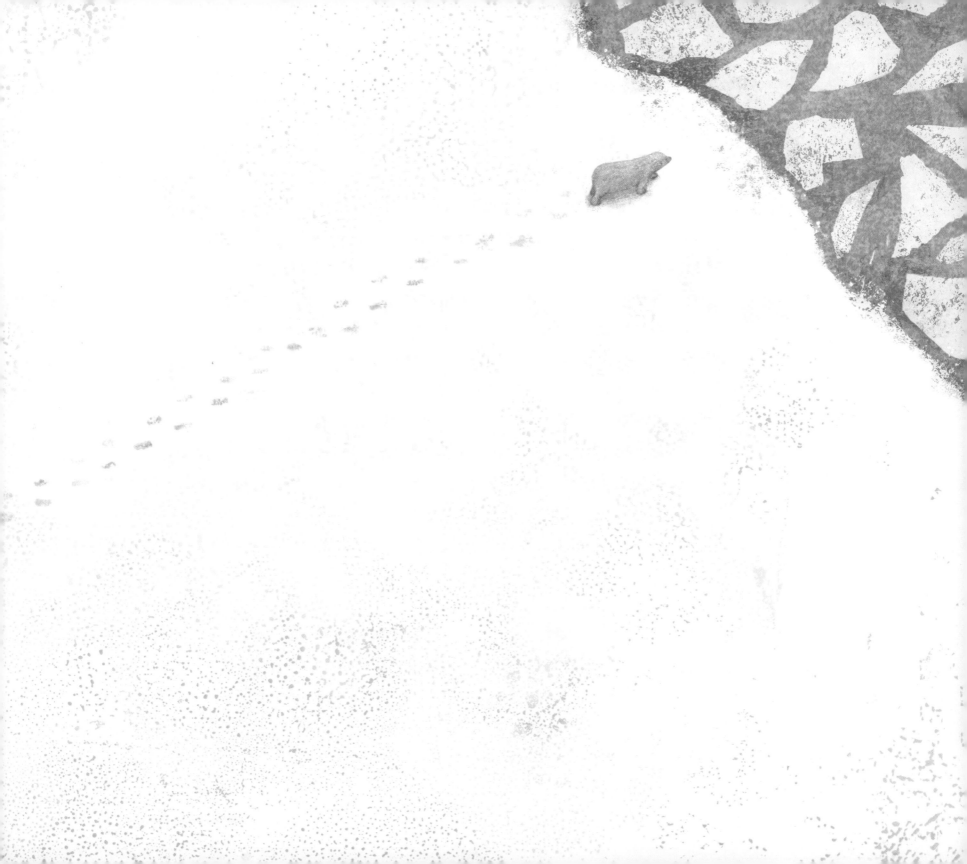

'Mum, where are you?'

A shape in the sea.
Could it really be . . .

'Mum!'

No paddling left in little legs:
Mum swam Miki to a safer spot.
He wanted to tell her all about the Dot.

But it would have to wait.
Miki dived deep,
deep into sleep.